WHO TOLD THE MOST INCREDIBLE STORY?

THE SINGING COMPETITION AND OTHE

Naana J.E.S. Opoku-Agyemang

VOLUME 3

 Afram Publications (Ghana) Limited

Published by:
Afram Publications (Ghana) Limited
P.O. Box M18
Accra, Ghana

Tel:	+233 302 412 561, +233 244 314 103
Kumasi:	+233 322 047 524/5
E-mail:	sales@aframpubghana.com
	publishing@aframpubghana.com
Website:	www.aframpubghana.com

First Published, 2015
ISBN: 9964 70 535 2

Edited by: Adwoa A. Opoku-Agyemang
Illustrated by: Peter "Poka" Asamoa

Content   Page

EVERYONE DESERVES A HEARING

Why is it very important to listen to all sides of a case before we make up our minds or pass judgement? Sometimes the story of one person may sound so convincing that it annuls the need for another version. This is especially true when the informant is someone we know and trust. But how many times have we not changed our minds after everyone involved in that particular case has spoken! This is a true story which confirms what I mean that everyone, even an alleged murderer, deserves a hearing. So, remove the wax from your ears, listen carefully to my tale and pass it on...

A long time ago, there lived a King, Nana Ansa, who was much loved by his people. Unlike other Kings who arrogantly treated their subjects as slaves and pawns, Nana Ansa rightly saw his authority as coming directly from his people, and he treated them with a lot of respect. He also carried himself with the dignity befitting a king. The disgrace and contempt that pursued some rulers in other lands did not spread to the paramountcy of Nana Ansa because he gave no cause for such events. Some rulers persistently slept with the wives of others, misused public property or showed contempt for the opinion of their counsellors. Other rulers who were eventually removed from authority were those who perverted justice or who inflicted extortive fines and penalties on their subjects. Indeed, in these and other important matters, Nana Ansa was used as the measuring rod by others, particularly during chieftaincy disputes. All this brings me to what happened in Bosu many seasons ago.

The people of Bosu proferred charges against their king, who was eventually removed from power. Among other causes for discontent including persistent drunkenness and disorderly conduct, the chief of Bosu was charged with holding the umbrella over another chief. At another time, he was seen heckling over the price of venison. All of these charges came after futile attempts had been made to steer him onto the correct path. Before the sentence was passed, the degraded king was asked to learn from Nana Ansa whose fame had spread far indeed.

Nana Ansa had initiated several projects in his own town, including communal farms and providing incentives for teaching the youth some trades. It was difficult for his subjects not to participate in communal labour because the king was always the first to arrive at the site to be cleared or at the house to be repaired, and he was among the last to leave.

It so happened that Nana Ansa had a son, called Kwamena. Although the king had many children he was especially fond of Kwamena, whom he had apprenticed to the chief medicine man of the land. Kwamena was such an intelligent boy that he learnt very fast, surpassing the older students he had joined at the training post. Thanks to a sharp memory and keen sense of observation, he came to know the medicinal values of leaves, roots and barks. He could tell by the shape, age, colour and the rate by which a leaf became moist after rubbing it between the palms, for example, the disease it could cure. He was always right. And despite his social status as the son of the king, Kwamena was very respectful of others. He never forgot what his mother told him one day, that it takes a long time to come up in life and no time at all to come down, and that one loses nothing by showing respect to people. Commenting on his credentials, some of the elders wished he were a nephew, so that he could inherit his father; the members of his clan were matrilineal.

One day the chief medicine man sent Kwamena and a few other assistants to the forest to bring home some leaves which they had left in the shade to dry. After collecting the leaves, the youth wandered in different directions of the forest, looking at tree barks and predicting their medicinal values. It was during that field trip that Kwamena saw a palm tree which had fallen to the ground. He noticed that a white substance was leaking from the bark. He tasted the liquid and found it to be very sweet.

He immediately thought of sharing the drink with his father who was his best friend. When he saw the dried and hollowed out shell of the pumpkin fruit, he attached the mouth of the gourd to the trunk of the tree with palm fronds and continued with his mission of studying barks and leaves.

At the close of the day he went to the tree and found the gourd almost full with the sweet drink. He took the container and went to his father who had just finished presiding over the case of a subject who had accused another of sorcery. Kwamena showed the drink to his father who tasted it and immediately loved it. He left the drink for his father and went back to join his fellow apprentices who had planned to spend the evening making new straw sleeping mats.

The more Nana Ansa savoured the drink, the more he liked it. What he did not know was that the wine acquired potency very fast. Exhausted by the day's

activities and feeling thirsty, the king drank all of the wine and soon, a wave of relaxation flowed through his veins. His head felt light, and only the pleasant

6

things in his life came to his mind. The scenes of his installation, his marriage to Kwamena's mother, the absence of crime and the high communal spirit in his land flashed before him in an illogical sequence. At one point he could have sworn he saw the wall move, and along with it the leopard skin and swords. Then he shut his eyes, or rather his eyes shut by themselves, and there before him, were his wife and linguist getting married with everyone watching! He seemed to be the only one unhappy with the event. Then he found himself at the bank of the river, with a boatful of fish which others were stealing; he tried to shout for help but no words came out of his mouth…

It was the head of the army who first knocked on the door of the king and, receiving no answer, went home. Then came the linguist. He needed to confer with the king over a problem about a witness who was proving difficult in a land dispute. He also knocked for a while, and hearing no response, he decided to wait in the courtyard until the king woke up. When the king's wife, Kwamena's mother, brought his food and found him still sleeping, she expressed concern to the linguist. It was an odd time of the day for Nana to nap, and to sleep so deeply. Both of them went to the room and found their beloved king in such a deep sleep that no amounts of shouts could wake him. The two of them raised an alarm which brought the counsellors, elders, criers and messengers to the scene.

The immediate conclusion was that the king had been poisoned, because the manner in which he slept was most unusual. To make things worse, Nana would open his eyes which had acquired a glassy look, and he would make incomprehensible noises. Unfortunately, in the rare moments he made any sense he would be using the filthiest language ever heard. I cannot repeat those words to you. Drunkenness is a bad habit, you must believe me. But let me get on with the story. Yes, as I was telling you, Nana Ansa was drunk, a state of being he had never experienced before. He would stare at his hands, laugh long and hard when there was no cause for it, and when the people tried to sit him up in bed, the once dignified king vomited all over himself and those who tried to help.

The stench was abominable. The only plausible conclusion was the one reached earlier on, that the spiritual and moral leader had been poisoned. That was high treachery and the culprit had to be found and brought to justice.

The elders calmed down and went over the day's events, very slowly. Nothing unusual had occurred, and when they left the king after the case of sorcery, he was in good health. Unless the sorcerer had turned his magic on him? But how could be that be when the case was judged in his favour? They then searched the room and found a gourd with a stench very similar to the rankness which filled the room. Indeed, the king had been poisoned, but who could have thought that the man had any enemies? While all of this was going on the king fell back to a deep, deep sleep.

It then came to light that the only person who had been to the king since the court case was his son Kwamena. A couple of the elders who nursed their own jealousy of Kwamena were quick to find the young man, sitting and chatting with his friends. Without even finding out what had exactly happened, the elders called the executioners and ordered that Kwamena be killed, and so he was, before he had time to ask the nature of his crime. His head was brought on a wooden platter to the palace.

While the resulting wailing and commotion were going on, the king woke from his deep sleep and added to the confusion when he came out of the room, because he had been given up for dead. When the king saw the linguist he gave him an ominous look and asked for the mother of Kwamena, at which request the confusion was escalated. Pandemonium broke loose as the crowd fled, convinced of having seen a ghost. In his booming voice Nana Ansa called for calm and an explanation. The linguist moved cautiously towards the king and touched him; to make sure that he was solid. Convinced that he was indeed the king, the linguist narrated the episode and ended it by showing the head of Kwamena to Nana Ansa.

"Gods of the land, Linguist, why didn't you ask him to explain what he had given me?" With these words the king collapsed and died. He was buried the same day as his son. As for Kwamena's mother, she lived much longer, as the woman who always carried several things about her and who the children grew to call, in a sing song manner: 'Did you ask him? Why didn't you ask him?'

Must we not always listen to everyone's tale before we pass judgement?

THE TRUE REMEDY FOR GRIEF

Along with his fame and the high level of respect he commanded, Kweku Ananse the spider had also acquired a lot of enemies. These enemies were mainly those animals whose own inadequacies were enhanced by the achievements of the spider. Instead of spending time sharpening their own rusty intellect, these dopes rather contrived various plots by which they hoped to bring Ananse into disrepute. Matters reached a head when the king of the animals appointed Ananse to the enviable position of supreme counsellor.

Some of the animals disputed the manner of appointment and when this got them nowhere they suggested the names of other candidates like Elephant, Monkey and Snake who, they believed, could do an equally good job. These animals knew deep in their hearts that Ananse was the best person for the job, but they opposed him anyway, out of mere spite. The king silenced them all by saying that he had the prerogative to make such an appointment. He went on to remind them of the weaknesses of the other animals of their choice. And so Kweku Ananse became supreme counsellor.

At a meeting which was called to discuss matters relating to communal work,
the jealous animals upset the whole agenda by an amendment to the appointment

of supreme counsellor. The reform stipulated that whenever the supreme counsellor failed to give sound advice, he should first be demoted them humiliated, and finally, be killed. So intense was their hatred of Ananse that they would do everything in their power to trip up and eliminate him. At this particular meeting, Ananse argued all he could against the motion, seeing the act as barbarous and a deterrent to public peace. He cited instances in the history of the forest to support his claim that such measures had only succeeded in promoting mediocrity; what he meant was that if a counsellor were to be killed because he had made a bad decision, then it meant that no animal could grow on the job, for example. In his own experience, Ananse continued passionately, the more cases a counsellor handled, the better he or she became at the job.

The king knew that Ananse was right but he was secretly afraid of the other courtiers and hangers-on whom he had no will to dismiss; these were the most vociferous and the most spiteful. The king ruled in favour of the other animals.

Ananse went home a very worried man indeed. He did not fear for his life – that was not the issue – but that the king should be ruled by these vaunting animals who did not care about the future of the land. It was his wife Okondor who

17

reminded him that there is a price to pay for everything, even for excellence, but, she went on, as long as Ananse was not breaking any rules, he should just do his work as best he knew how. As for the amendment, she went on, it looked to her like the hole which is dug for the unsuspecting, but into which the digger always falls.

The animals left the palace of the king very happy. They knew that sooner or later Ananse would make a mistake, and on that happy day, they would all be relieved of a man who they were convinced thought that the rest of them were fools; they would show him that they came into the world before him. From the time of their victory, they spent the best part of their time finding difficult cases for Ananse to solve. Ananse however grew in wisdom as he found ways of getting round difficult situations. With time, the other animals became desperate.

One day, contrary to all rules of the forest, some of the animals went to the shrine of the neighbouring village and defecated on their gods. The king of that village declared war, and Ananse was called to counsel the king and the state. Ananse was able to find the culprits, and he advised that they be handed over to the king for sacrifice. The animals who perished through their own folly were Hen, Pheasant, Turkey, Goat, Sheep and Cow. Even then the other animals did not give up; they wanted to see Ananse repressed, disgraced and exterminated, according to the details of the amendment.

Then one day Elephant, the leader of the unmanageable, called the other lackeys to a meeting in the house of Donkey. You see, Elephant did not want the king to see that he was the architect of all the disturbances in the land; Elephant always managed to get Cat, Dog, Pig and Monkey to articulate and dramatize his diabolical plans. The other buffoons agreed to attend the rendezvous. At that gathering Elephant told them that Ostrich had lost all four of her babies in four days. They should go to the king and seek advice on how to console Ostrich.

Ostrich was called and schooled on how she should behave at the meeting. She was to insist on nothing but having her children back with her, alive. The others congratulated Elephant, thinking what a marvellous idea he had. So Elephant publicly called on Ostrich and asked her why she was weeping so inconsolably when there was a supreme counsellor in their midst. Ostrich was reminded, just in case she had forgotten, that a supreme counsellor was supposed to be intelligent enough to help the less intelligent get out of difficult situations. Elephant thus goaded Ostrich on to the palace to seek advice.

Things were so orchestrated that when Ostrich arrived at the mansion, all the other animals were already seated. Ostrich stood up and told the pathetic story of the death of her four babies, barely a week after their father had passed. She had so well rehearsed her tale that by the time she came to an end, the tears were streaming down the faces of some of the animals; others tried to shed tears in solidarity. It was a jubilant Elephant who spoke after Ostrich, calling on Ananse, in his singular position as supreme counsellor, to use his undisputed wisdom to bring the four babies of Ostrich back to life.

Ananse made Ostrich repeat her story, much to the delight of the others. They were convinced that on this occasion, they had managed to pin Ananse's back to the wall. Ananse had pity on Ostrich for two reasons, first for her sudden and painful losses, and secondly for allowing her plight to be handled in such a profane manner. Ananse kept quiet for a long time before he spoke:

"Ostrich, I have a solution to your problem; I can bring your children and their father back to life."

At this utterance some animals pulled their chairs closer, while others stretched their necks, just in order to take in everything that was being said by the supreme counsellor. Ananse saw the drama unfolding and he continued:

"I am aware of only one means by which the dead can be brought back to life...

It was Snake who interrupted Ananse: "Look, just tell us what it is, because the sorrowful mood of Ostrich is driving us all crazy."

"I am glad that you are interested, Snake. I like to see the cooperative spirit work amongst us, instead of the petty jealousies that threaten to destroy us."

"With all respect, Ananse, do get on with the solution," said Elephant. "Later on we can debate about the future of our beloved land."

"I was coming directly to that. What I need is simple: just a few mustard seeds," said Ananse.

"I have a whole sack full of mustard seeds," volunteered Snake who could hardly wait to see Ananse mess up. "You can have it all if..." This time it was Ananse who interrupted him, unable to bear his animosity any longer:

"The mustard seed should come from a home to which Death has never paid a visit."

As I conclude this story, the animals are still roaming from house to house; they have not yet found a home which has not experienced death.

WHAT WOULD YOU HAVE DONE?

Once upon a time, long, long ago, even before the great grandparents of the great grandparents of your great-grandfather and great-grandmother were born, there lived an old woman called Nana Adwoa. This old woman was very sad indeed because she had lost all her relatives and she had no human friends. She had several animals for friends though. These animals included Parrot, Tortoise, and Deer. They had a good relationship but they were acutely aware that Nana Ama would also like to have people around her. There were times, especially after the harvesting was done and there was not much work to do on the farm, when they would all spend some time together, telling stories of their adventures in the forest. Parrot told the story of how he had managed to free himself from some sticky gum left on a branch by a hunter:

"My friends, I felt I would not survive to tell the story! Wasn't I ever scared! Listen to my story and pass it on...After a good meal of palm nuts and a cool drink at the fountain I slowly pruned my feathers and flew over some tall trees, just to enjoy the beautiful scene. It is wonderful how many things one can see from the top of a tall tree. I could see the landscape very well, with the undulations of the land and the footpaths we had created. I also enjoyed looking at the state of farms. You know, some people know how to free their plants of weeds and leave enough spaces in between them to allow for a good yield, while others crops are in such locked combat with weeds that I often ask myself where the farmers had gone when the Sky God was distributing wisdom. That day, I could also see a snake track a mouse and that mouse was as determined not to become the snake's dinner."

"This is really what I envy," interrupted Tortoise. "Just look at me. I have always wondered why I can never climb a tree just in order to experience the joy of seeing so far into the distance".

Deer was the next to speak: "Tortoise, you must really do something about your habit of stressing your handicaps all the time. You are forever comparing yourself unfavourably with others. What do you get out of it? Just consider for a moment their own disadvantages. You must learn to be happy with yourself."

"I think we should get on with our stories. Don't forget that we will have to start clearing the land for planting, and very soon there will be no time for storytelling. Parrot, get on with the tale."

"Well," Parrot proceeded, "after I had rested for a while, I wanted to fly off to another part of the forest and that was when I discovered that I could not move. My feet were stuck to the branch! I realised that if I did not act fast I could end up, if I were lucky, in a cage as a pet repeating rude sentences and comments. I was too scared to even consider the worst fate of being transformed into a roasted delicacy."

"So how did you escape? You apparently did or else you would not be here." Deer was anxious all the same.

"I owe my life to the Red Ant," replied Parrot. "Red Ant heard my cries and came to my assistance"

"Parrot," interrupted Tortoise, "are you telling us that a grown person like you was actually crying? I mean bawling loud enough for people to hear you? Like a child who cannot control his or her emotions? Really?"

"What is the point of crying if he did not want others to hear him? And what has being a child got to do with the bad combination of fear and grief? Or haven't you followed the story? The man was in great difficulty. I mean his life was in danger. I am a grown man but I would have bawled too," Cat defended Parrot's public display of sentiment.

Everyone laughed at this because Cat is not very brave.

"Red Ant, perceiving the danger I was in," continued Parrot, "went and summoned all the members of his extended family. They were so many, yet they moved in a most orderly fashion. The bigger ones formed a protective wall at each side of the pathway, while the others marched in the middle. Once in a while, a leader would leave the side of the pathway in order to inspect the others at the back of the column, while another took a quick run to the front to make sure that everyone was going in the right direction. The sense of purpose was most impressive. Once they reached the branch where I was cemented, they set to task without delay. They slowly nibbled at the hardened glue and freed my feet from the sticky substance. Up to this day, I never forget to share my food with Red Ant and his family, as a sign of my gratitude. In fact, I am looking for other ways of making Red Ant and his family know that I truly still appreciate their love and concern."

Nana Adwoa sighed, then said, "Parrot, your tale about gratitude brings me to a very important part of my life, and I will now tell the story of how I ended up lost in the forest and denied of human company. Listen to my story, and pass it on...

I have not always lived by myself, without human company. In fact, once, I was all by myself just as I am now, and even then I did not have you for friends. I was wandering in the forest one day feeling really sorry for myself when I met Pigeon who felt even sorrier for me.

'Old Woman, what are you doing here, isolated from everyone?' asked Pigeon. 'Whenever I am flying I always find you alone, talking to yourself. What is your story?'

'Oh, my lady Pigeon, first of all thank you for taking an interest in me. I used to have a very big family, but I got a bad disease for which there was no cure, and afraid that they would also get it, my people abandoned me in this thick forest and now I cannot find my way back home. I miss my family very much, especially my granddaughter.'

'Your people are heartless indeed! Don't they know that human beings must be accepted no matter their circumstances and that the medicine men must find a remedy for diseases? If we start rejecting people because they have diseases we cannot cure, soon we will start hating others because they are disfigured, or because they have practices we cannot understand or even more stupid, because they simply look different. After all, no one has identical fingers on one hand.'

'Pigeon, I can understand how you feel, but which normal human being will be dumb enough to hate someone just because he looks different? That is really going too far. How can the variety in nature be appreciated if we all looked the same? Assuming all the birds looked the same, with the same size of beak and same arrangement of feathers and the same colour, the fishes the same shape and size, the trees the same height, with the same number of branches and same pattern of leaves, the flowers the same hue and at the same state of growth the monkeys...'

'Oh, well, I see the point but your people did not do well… Anyway, let me see what I can do to change your fortune.'

'Change my fortune? Pigeon, I would forever be grateful to you. All I want is to have human beings around me again. I miss the marriage ceremonies, the settlement of cases, the initiation rites, I miss the songs we compose as we smoke fish, and yes, I even miss the squabbles and the disasters, because they all helped us to know one another better and to find ways of living together again. Worst of all, I miss my granddaughter so much.'

'What is your name?' asked Pigeon.

'They call me Nana Adwoa because I am an old woman and I was born on a Monday, but I was named after the aunt of my father who did not have any children of her own and they did not want her to feel her name would die off because her only child had been drowned at sea when he was a young man…'

'That is enough. Can you identify the spot where we are? I want you to meet me here on Monday before the sun wakes up. Remember, today is Friday. Monday is your soul day and so we should have a lot of luck in changing your fortune.'

'Pigeon, how can I thank you? You have given me such hope!' I said, with tears in my eyes. 'I will do anything you ask of me.'

'All I need is for you to vouch for my safety and that of my children, after I have granted your wish,' Pigeon said earnestly.

'Is that all? I can protect you and your children without any difficulty whatsoever', I assured Pigeon. 'Just get me out of this wretched life and I will make sure that no pigeon ever comes to harm.'

We parted company, to meet at the appointed time and place. I did not know that three days took so long to arrive! I was beginning to feel that someone was playing games with time. I was so anxious I could hardly sleep. Barely a day after this meeting, I began to feel I had lost count of the days, and that it was Tuesday! I rambled in the forest until late in the evening when I met Moth who told me it was only Saturday. That helped a bit, but not too much. I was still so anxious that I slept a strange kind of sleep. You know, that deep kind of sleep which lasts a short while. When I woke up, it was still Saturday.

Anyway, on Sunday night, I went and slept at the spot where we had agreed to meet, in order not to be late. Pigeon arrived early, when it was still dawn and the air was damp with the morning dew. She had a small old bag made of straw, dangling from her beak.

'Good morning, Pigeon. I am so glad you came. As I was telling you the last time...'

Pigeon put her wing over her beak, meaning I should keep quiet. She stood still for a while, then she took out a small bottle of gin and performed libation, calling on both my ancestors and hers to witness the event and to direct it to a successful end. After the prayer, she tasted the gin and signalled me to do the same. Then she directed me to follow her. We danced around the silk cotton tree three times, after which she took a couple of palm kennels from her small bag. She held the first one and said:

'May her appearance be changed.'

Suddenly, my torn cloth was gone. I was clothed in rich kente and velvet, with a beautiful pair of sandals on my feet.

I had gold necklaces and Aggrey beads woven in intricate designs around my wrist and ankles. When I touched my hair I could feel the royal haircut and head gear. I had to suppress my delight because Pigeon wanted silence until she indicated otherwise.

'May houses and trees appear,' continued Pigeon.

No sooner were these words out of her mouth than, the forest turned into a town, with good strong houses, wonderfully plastered and decorated. There were so many houses of different shapes and sizes that I could not guess the number or where they ended. There were roads and pathways, and many trees and plants as well. There were mango, avocado pear, guava, orange, banana, pawpaw and other fruit trees which I could not recognise immediately. At the centre of the town was the old silk cotton tree under which I was standing, with Pigeon.

When Pigeon said, 'May animals appear,' goats, sheep, pigs, chickens, turkeys, ducks and pheasants of various ages and sizes roamed the town like they had been there all the time.

Then Pigeon turned to me and said, 'I am going to people this town, and you will be the Queen. Just remember to keep my children and I safe at all costs, or you will return to your former state. My children and I will live in this silk cotton tree, close to your palace. Don't breathe a word about what has just taken place to anyone. Your indebtedness will show itself in how you keep your word. Good luck.'

As Pigeon flew to the top of the tree, she said, 'May people come.' Suddenly, the houses had people living in them. There were old men, old women, young people, and children going about their business as it used to happen in my old village. Two women were counting smoked fish and arranging them in a pattern in a huge basket, which was secured by an old fishing net, soon to be set on its way to other parts of the land. A man was weaving cloth, his feet moving in rhythm with his hands as he sang a song to help with his concentration. He had on display strips of woven cloth and larger pieces as well. A carpenter was in his workshop making furniture while his apprentices looked on; there were boards of odum, sapele, mahogany, wawa and others lying in the corner of his workshop.

There were of course gold and silversmiths busy at melting their ores and casting. I could also see a medicine woman at work, pounding herbs in a mortar and talking to the patients who had come to her for treatment. Then I heard a group of musicians drumming towards me. In front of the retinue were singers, singing my praises and inviting me back to the palace.

"You know, it almost felt like the old times before I got sick, with my family around me again. However, there was a huge difference: this time I was Queen. I had a lot of power; I was rich and very happy. The happiest event of all was to have my granddaughter with me again. She always ate with me from the same bowl, made me tell her stories and slept in my bed. My work as a Queen was easy because I had counsellors who were well versed in the laws of the land and who settled the few conflicts that arose even before I was informed of them. I was indeed very happy, and I always kept in my mind the promise I made to Pigeon, until tragedy struck.

Mm! my people, my granddaughter was taken seriously ill. At first, we tried the herbs that we all knew about, in order to bring down her temperature, but the fever kept raging on. I was so afraid of losing her entirely or having her come out of her convulsions as a damaged person. I summoned a medicine man from another town; he was renowned all over the land. He told us not to worry because his own neighbour's child had had a similar problem and he had cured it without any difficulty. He left a balm to be rubbed on the child's body, three times in the day. The fever abated for about three days and just as we were all about to forget about the sickness, she had a terrible spell of the fever again, and this time, it was much worse than ever before.

My granddaughter grew so feeble that we were all afraid she would die. My anguish knew no end. Finally, we consulted the medicine woman of the town. She said she had heard of the fever that would not be appeased and was surprised she had not been called earlier. She went on that it was not an ordinary fever but the symptom of a bigger disease, and that she knew the cure. We all breathed a sigh of relief and I offered her gold dust just for the assurance. She declined the gift and said she only took payment after the patient was completely healed.

Then, my people, what do you think this woman wanted to prepare the medicine to heal my granddaughter with, but the blood of baby pigeons!"

"Ei! Ei! Old Woman, you were in real difficulty!" said Deer.

"My mother's child, what a trial," wailed Tortoise.

"This is like taking in snuff at the beach!" Parrot summed up the situation.

"Yes, indeed it was like having to make a choice where there was no choice. As soon as the medicine woman asked for the blood of the baby pigeons, my son-in-law, Antobam, got up and offered to bring them down from the silk cotton tree. Then I told him he could not do that.

'With all respect, Nana, what do you mean?' asked Antobam, finding it difficult to understand my order.

I ignored him for a while and turned to the medicine woman: 'My lady, please find another ingredient for the cure. I will provide anything else that you want and pay any price, but I cannot sacrifice the babies of Pigeon.'

The medicine woman looked long and hard at me and said she wanted to ask for permission to attend to her other patients and we could call her when we had found the baby pigeons, because there was no other known cure.

I continued to insist that we could not use the baby pigeons and so I ordered the talking drums to be sounded, to call together all the medicine men of the land. They all came and gave different prescriptions, but to no avail.

After three days, my granddaughter had stopped eating; her body was emaciated and she was breathing like the dying. Added to this, my daughter and my son-in-law had accused me of witchcraft and said I was responsible for the child's ill health. That was the only way in which they could understand why I would refuse to have pigeons sacrificed to save a human life, and my own granddaughter's, for that matter. My counsellors started making moves to remove me from the throne and to have me tried for witchcraft. For the first time, people stopped greeting me in the streets; instead, they behaved as if I were a transmittable disease. They did not just avoid me; they made me realise I was not wanted. The hostility was so intense that I could literally feel it. And to think I was their Queen! Even the village fool openly called me names and asked the worth of a Queen who kills her own relations. Then the chief priest told us all one day that if the child died, there would be famine and untold disasters. While all of this was going on, Pigeon flew by more regularly than ever, evidently to remind me of my promise.

My friends, what would you have done?"

THE SINGING COMPETITION

Once upon a time, Onyankopon the Sky God summoned all the animals in his kingdom and told them that he would offer a most handsome reward to the animal with the most melodious voice. The winner would be determined after an open musical contest. Apart from the cash reward, the winner would also live in the palace of God and be employed in the envious position of court singer and entertainer. The animals were very pleased at the chance to show off their talents and the possibility of a change in career. Most of the animals had heard of the splendour of the palace of God, and this was their chance to actually experience it. I am sure you would also love to live in an environment pleasantly different from yours, wouldn't you? Well, let me get on with the story. At the end of the meeting, Onyankopon set the date for the event.

The forest burst into melodious activity in response to this announcement. A lot of the animals wanted to enter this competition and were all determined to make a good impact. As I walked to my farm I could hear singing of all kinds, either in solo or in choral form. Some sang in soprano, alto, or bass, while others showed dexterity in combining the various ways in which a voice can express itself. Those who had previously not exercised their vocal chords with consistency and seriousness could be heard making desperate efforts to remove the rust from their voices, while those who had been known to practise regularly stepped up their efforts.

Some of the animals believed that bananas had a good effect on the vocal chords and so they ate nothing else. Those who thought groundnuts did the trick put themselves on a strict diet of roasted, boiled or candied nuts. Others swore by cola nuts and so they braved the bitter taste, eating them in abundance and enjoying the sweet aftertaste when they drank water. Those who did not wish to leave any stone unturned, actually chewed both kinds of nuts and ate the bananas also. All this took place while they very actively practised daily. Such was the high level of determination.

At last the expected day arrived, and you should have been there! You know, some things are better experienced that heard recounted. Anyway, I was there, and so allow me to do my best to share the experience with you. As I was saying, I had

49

a very good time. The animals tried frantically, as they took their turn one after the other, to make an impression. Dog was the first to begin this important contest. He walked to the middle of the circle demarcated for the competition, raised his neck and allowed the air to flow through his throat as his way of singing.

Neither the posture nor the outcome took him very far because the song was too monotonous. When Crow took the stand, the audience literally looked for a place to hide, wondering if he was daring the world to come crashing on their heads. Crow was advised to stop singing because such a voice as he had was enough to scare even the most daring person away from the palace of God. Snake hissed away by way of demonstrating his musical ability. The verdict? That Onyankopon wanted an entertaining voice, not one that had the potential to cause nightmares even in adults. By the time Sheep and Goat started bleating, the judges wondered if it was a good idea to have allowed everyone to enter the competition. They were determined to design a format to shortlist contestants the next time round. The judges and audience found the screeching of Cricket too irritating, the buzzing of Bee too unsettling, the croaking of Frog too annoying and the whining of Fly most unsuitable for the objective of the contest. At the end of the day, no animal had qualified for the prize.

This was the time Kweku Ananse the spider, who had been watching the competition from a distance, got his idea. He went to Onyankopon and told him that if he would give him three days, he would come prepared to try to win the position of singer and entertainer in the palace of God. Determined to hire the services of an

entertainer, Onyankopon agreed to this request and dismissed the judges and the audience, to reassemble three days later.

Ananse went straight into the bushes, in search of the bird with the most pleasant voice. He listened carefully to the singing of many birds, and finally settled on the canary whose voice he felt would do the trick. Ananse told Canary, who for a strange reason had not heard of the singing competition, that the frog was boasting he could sing better than her, and that he, Ananse, wanted to prove Frog wrong. Canary was offended by Frog's effrontery:

"Ah, that animal who has no idea of his own length! And I have often wondered how his voice sounds even in his own ears. How dare he compare his croaks to my melodious voice!" Canary chirped with indignation.

"Indeed, Canary, I knew you would be upset about such a thing. The reason for all of this is that some animals believe him and have contributed to a competition between the two of you, and the winner will get a lot of gold. Lion is backing Frog, and I have decided to do the most sensible thing, to give out my support."

"This is strange indeed. What does Lion think he is doing? What animal will place money on such a bet when it is very clear what the outcome will be? Anyway, since my honour is at stake, I will willingly enter the competition and remove all doubt." Canary thus assured Ananse.

"There is something you should know about the procedure in order to make it fair: the patrons have a role to play in the competition. Therefore Frog will hide

in Lion's sack while you hide in my pocket. And as soon as I pat my pocket, you must begin to sing. But there is one thing you need to do."

"Just let me know so that not only will I put Frog to shame, I will also become rich and famous."

"You must let me know both the tune and the lyrics in advance," Ananse told Canary.

Canary agreed to the rules and sang her song for Ananse to memorise. Then she set off with Ananse for the contest.

When Ananse got to the palace grounds he found Onyankopon seated with the judges, ready to listen to his song. When Ananse arrived, he removed the part of his cloth that covered his left shoulder as a sign of respect, and tapped his pocket, whereupon Canary began to sing.

Ananse mouthed along with the voice of Canary, and did it so well that no one could tell he was just miming the lyrics. At the end of the song Onyankopon came down from his throne and embraced Ananse, pronouncing him the court singer and entertainer, and handed him a bag of gold dust. Ananse thanked the God and his judges and went home.

Hardly were they home than Canary asked what had actually happened because she had not heard Frog sing. "Oh, I forgot to tell you that each contestant was to sing alone. When we arrived, Frog had already sung. And had been booed out of the palace grounds, and that is why you did not hear him."

"Well, that is not important. Now I want my money, so that I can return to my family," Canary told Ananse.

However, Ananse was trying to find a way of keeping the earnings all to himself, so he told Canary to be patient and wait for a couple of days while he sorted a few things out. Every time Canary asked for her money Ananse would find an excuse, until it slowly dawned on Canary that Ananse had made a big fool out of her. This is one thing I find it so difficult to believe about some people. I know none of you will be as selfish and as uncaring as Kweku Ananse was, especially on this occasion. He really would have gained a lot of the warmth and friendship, not forgetting about Canary's trust, if only he had shared the prize with her. You should all beware of that awful motivator called greed. So you can understand why Canary also quietly planned her revenge, and how the newly-rich and respected Kweku Ananse was publicly humiliated.

Ananse felt happy that Canary had stopped harassing him for her money and had even settled into the role of his housekeeper. So good was Canary at keeping house that when Ananse moved into the palace of God as singer and entertainer, he went with Canary, so that he could enjoy complete leisure. Ananse was still too greedy to part with even a small piece of the enormous treasure he had 'won' during the competition, so he gave Canary nothing.

One day God received tribute from all his creatures, and he decided to entertain them with music after the feasting, which had lasted three days and three nights. After wonderful sessions of drum, flute, and horn music, the great court entertainer and singer, Kweku Ananse, was called to prove his merit. Ananse was so happy that he had Canary with him. She readily agreed to hide in his pocket and sing as usual. What Ananse did not know was that Canary saw this occasion as her chance to get even.

Ananse put on one of the fine cloths that came with his prize, and, with Canary hiding in his pocket, he got ready to sing. As usual he tapped his pocket, but this time Canary kept mute. Ananse tapped again, but he again received no response: Canary refused to sing. From gentle pats Ananse started patting very hard, until, unable to endure the slaps any longer, Canary flew out of Ananse's pocket, perched on the branch of a nearby tree, and sang the most beautiful songs the audience had ever heard, ending with the one that won Ananse the position and wealth.

Then Canary told her story of the deception and treachery of Ananse. Onyankopon immediately took back all his treasures while the audience hooted at Ananse. Kweku Ananse was so ashamed that he looked to his left, then to his right, and then jumped to hide at the corner of the roof.

WHY THE CAT ALWAYS CHASES THE MOUSE

"Nana," Adwoa called her grandmother, "you promised to tell us a story this evening. I have finished my work and I have also bathed." "You have always helped around the house, Adwoa, and I am very happy about that. But you must find out if Kweku and Kwabena have finished burning the dried grass and if they have bathed, then I will tell a story."

Shortly afterwards the three children came with their stools and sat around Nana. They arranged to sit in such a way as to rest their heads on Nana's thighs. They found this to be a most comfortable way of listening to the story; sometimes they would fall asleep before the story ended. Today, Nana had promised to tell a story to explain why the cat always chases the mouse...

"We may as well wonder," Nana started," if the cat and the mouse have eternally had this awful relationship with the cat forever chasing the mouse, and with the mouse having to find ingenious ways of avoiding the cat..."

"What really happened?" asked Kwabena.

"How did they become lasting enemies?" enquired Kweku.

"Has the Cat ever been friends with the Mouse?" Adwoa wanted to know.

"The elders say that when the musicians are drumming towards your father's house, you must not rush into the street to hear the music." Nana said, by way of telling her grandchildren to patiently wait for the story.

"The elder is anyone older than you, Nana?" Adwoa felt that her grandmother was very old indeed.

"I don't hear any music, and I want to hear about the cat and the mouse" said Kwabena, the meaning of the proverb flying right over his head. Kweku was older and understood by the proverb that their interruptions were delaying the telling of the story: "What Grandmother means is that we should cut in less and simply listen."

"Kweku is so right," said Nana, "let us find out why the cat and the mouse never became friends again:

"Long, long ago, Cat, Mouse and Dog were friends. They lived in the same house, had the same farm and even ate from the same bowl during meal times. That is how close they were.

So how did division find itself into such a close relationship? It is all the fault of Dog. How? Well listen on and don't keep the story to yourself.

"Cat's job was to go to the market during the lean season and buy the food items because she was very good at bargaining. Mouse and Dog did the cooking, because they were good cooks. When the food was ready they would all sit down and eat from the same bowl.

"Meanwhile, although Dog was a good cook he was also very lazy; in fact Dog was the laziest animal on the land. He took advantage of his size in intimidating Mouse to do most of the cooking. It got to a point where Mouse was doing all the cooking. As soon as it was time to cook Dog would just lie at the corner, order Mouse about and when he was not talking he would breathe loudly through his mouth, with the saliva rolling off his tongue, painting a scene which greatly annoyed Mouse.

"Dog was the first to tell when the food was ready, and he would get up, wash his hands and get ready to enjoy a meal he had not helped to prepare.

"The problem with Mouse was that he never protested about Dog's habit."

"Maybe he was afraid," said Kweku, "you know Dog is bigger than Mouse."

"You are right, Kweku, but even when people who are bigger or stronger than we are take advantage of us, we must never fail to find a way of letting them know how we feel," said Maame Mansa who had joined them.

"This is exactly what happened," continued Nana. "One day Mouse decided he had had enough and would teach Dog a lesson:

"'I will make sure Dog does not continue taking me for a fool,' Mouse muttered under his breath. "'If he thinks I will cook for him every day then he has something else coming.'

"That day when Cat brought the vegetables and dried fish from the market, Mouse washed the vegetables and the fish and soon started cooking. After the dried beans, hot pepper and egg plant had been cooked separately he broke the fish into large pieces, salted them lightly and placed them in the pot. Then he peeled and sliced onions and placed them on top of the fish. After he had added a couple

65

of tomatoes to the fish and the onions he covered the pot and left it on the fire to cook. He then peeled the cassava and the plantains and boiled them together, with the cassava at the bottom of the pot. As usual, Dog stretched his neck over his forepaws, just observing Mouse as if Mouse were giving a presentation. When the soup was simmering and he had started pounding the plantain and the cassava Mouse told Dog:

"'Good friend Dog.'

"'Good friend Mouse, I am listening'.

"'I almost forgot to tell you that your brother was here while you took a nap'.

"'Oh! Was he? I must have dozed off. Why didn't you wake me up?' asked Dog.

"'You know, that was just when Cat had brought the produce from the market and I had started washing the vegetables. I thought you wanted to rest at the usual time when I did the cooking.'

"'Did he leave any message? I haven't had the time to visit them for a while,' said Dog, who did not detect the irony in Mouse's voice.

"'I was coming to that. He said you must come without delay and listen to an important but frightening decision taken by your council over the payment of family dues,' Mouse informed him.

"'I can well imagine the stupid litigation into which they have placed everyone once again. Certainly I can't go now. It will soon be lunch time and I am already hungry,' Dog whimpered.

"'I would go immediately if I were you. Your family truly respects your decisions. Moreover, you have consistently complained about the head of your family. If you do not go you may find yourself paying intolerable dues. Don't worry about the food. You know we always eat together. We will either wait for you or leave your share.'

"When the food was ready, Mouse invited Cat to share the meal.

"'Where is Dog?

'Didn't he tell you? He said he was going on a journey and so he would miss lunch.'

'Dog missing lunch? That is news!' Cat said.

"'Well it's an emergency.'

"'Why, is someone dead?'

"'No, nothing as bad as that. His family has reached an impasse again over family dues.'

"'Never heard of a family that must constantly fight over the most common of practices like paying dues,' said Cat. 'We had better leave Dog his portion and eat ours because I am really starving.'

"As soon as they had finished eating and were about to wash their hands, in came Dog panting, having run all the way from a meeting that never took place. He was really angry, and wondered what Mouse was up to.

"'Dog, Mouse told me you had travelled. Where did you go?' asked Cat.

"'I will tell you later. Mouse, where is my food?' Mouse had divided the produce which Cat brought from the market into three and had cooked only his portion and Cat's. So he gave Dog his portion of uncooked food.

"'This should not be so difficult,' said Cat, after all you are such a good, fast cook.'

"'I think there is some firewood left. You have to go to Donkey's house and get some live coals to light it,' Mouse directed Dog.

"Dog was really furious but he could not complain because he felt that somehow he deserved the treatment Mouse was giving him. Yet while he cooked his food, he hatched a plot for vengeance.

"Soon after this incident Cat gave birth to a beautiful baby. However, Cat lived very far away from her relations, and so Mouse offered to help her to take care of the baby. In the night when the baby cried, Mouse would wake up and rock him back to sleep, so that Cat would not feel so tired. In the daytime Mouse would also bathe the baby and play with him. Meanwhile Dog would sleep through the night and offer no help at all during the day. Cat decided just to ignore Dog and entrust her baby with Mouse, whose help she appreciated enormously.

"As I have already told you, Dog had plans about revenge which he kept in his head, waiting for the right moment. One day, after Cat had gone to the market and her baby had been particularly difficult, Mouse finally managed to calm the baby who presently slept. Exhausted, he also decided to have a siesta.

"While both Mouse and the baby slept, Dog said: 'this is my chance!'

"Dog climbed the window and entered the room quietly, carefully picked the baby and trotted off into the forest where he hid the sleeping baby.

"He came back home and placed himself at the same spot he had occupied when Cat was leaving for the market.

"Before long, Cat came home and left the basket of food in the kitchen. Sensing that the room was quiet, she decided to have a quick bath because she wanted to be clean and fresh while she nursed her baby. After her bath she went to her room to get dressed. That was when she discovered her baby was not lying at his sleeping place.

"'Mouse! Where is my baby?'

"'My God! I did not know I had fallen asleep.'

"'Fallen asleep indeed!' she catcalled. When I first entered the room I thought you were dead! How can a babysitter sleep the sleep of death? Someone could have come into the room and packaged you off for all you cared. But where in the name of the Gods is my baby?'

"'Your baby was lying right here. I fed him and put him to sleep, right here'

"'Right where? I say where is my baby? I trusted you with my baby. Where is he?'

"'Oh! Where is the baby?'

"'That's my question! Now, you had better answer me!'

"'Well, I left him lying right here.

"'Mouse, don't mistake my patience for stupidity,' she growled, advancing aggressively towards Mouse. Her tail stood up in the air, her entire coat on end. Mouse had never seen Cat so wrathful and he had not even known Cat's fur would join in the expression of fury.

"Dog certainly did not make any effort to restore peace between the two friends. As usual, he lay on the ground, stretched his neck over his hands and breathed through his mouth as if the scene were perfectly normal.

"'I left... the baby... lying... right... there...'

"With these words Mouse started to inch towards the door and finally, he fled for his life, hounded by Cat.

"So if today Cat chases the Mouse, it is because of Dog's evil plan."

BETWEEN WEALTH AND KINDNESS

A long time ago, the people who lived in a village called Biakoye were very close, even closer than we are now. They showed a lot of concern for each other's' plights and they generally looked out for each other. In those days people did not lock their doors because there was no need to. No one took what did not belong to him, without first asking the owner's permission. Of course the few rogues who broke the rules were chased out of the community. But the distinctive characteristics of the people were the love and concern they had for each other. This, of course, meant that people had to give a lot of their time and their wealth too, to help others in less fortunate circumstances. However, it was not everyone who was keen on giving without counting the cost.

Two such people who made a clean choice at one point in their lives between wealth and human kindness were Dogo and Bonto. These two men were rich but they were also very selfish; they would only help if they were going to get services of equal measure in return. They felt that all poor people were just lazy, and that the community's way of readily coming to the aid of people in need did not encourage the poor to help themselves. They decided that since they could provide for all their needs, they could afford to ignore everyone else's.

The inhabitants of the village watched them as these kept to themselves and only socialized with people of similar economic status. Dogo and Bonto completely underestimated the resentment of the rest of the community. Nowhere did this dislike become clearer than when the two young men decided it was time for them to get married. They felt that their wealth would easily pave the way for them, until they were effectively snubbed by one poor family after the other. Neither Dogo nor Bonto could understand why the poor were not keen on allowing the rich to bestow the privilege of wealth on them through marriage. Their rich friends did not welcome their proposals either, seeing that the suitors could offer nothing beyond what they owned. It became clear that they had to seek brides from outside the village, which they did, and performed their marriage rites and ceremonies with ample display of wealth and pageantry. No one from their village was willing to accompany them to the marriage ceremonies, and so when they returned to their village, the two wealthy men moved to build their houses far away from the poor people, and so lived on the outskirts of the village. They built bougainvillea hedges around their houses and kept wild dogs to frighten any of the villagers who would come to pluck any of their fruit. They would sit in their balconies and enjoy the spectacle of their dogs chasing frightened children who had come to collect ripe mangos or guavas from their trees, or who had simply been attracted to the houses by their agreeable appearance.

They enjoyed their blissful life until barely a year after their marriages, when news arrived about the death of Dogo's mother-in-law. That was serious business, because no one went to the funeral of an in-law alone. Dogo needed a whole contingent of people to accompany him to mourn his mother-in-law. The only person he associated with was Bonto, and although money was not the problem, people were. When they approached their rich neighbours they all said they were too busy to waste time on funerals. Dogo and Bonto thought for a long time about

what to do, and at first they ruled out the possibility of approaching the elders of the village, in view of the strained relationship between them. On the other hand, there was no way of showing up at the funeral all by themselves.

After much thinking and arguing, the two men realised that they had to swallow their pride and approach the chief for help. When the chief received messengers bearing expensive drinks from the two rich men who had ignored the villagers' appeal for help in the past, he knew something serious was going on, so he summoned his counsellors to devise a plan of action. The chief sent notice to Dogo and Bonto that their drinks had been well received and that they could approach the council with their supplication. The two rich, selfish friends were delighted. They wore their best cloths, went to the palace of the chief, and placed their request before the council of elders.

The chief assured them that they would get the help they required in their time of need, because, as they were very well aware, the village had always chosen people above wealth. But Dogo and Bonto should satisfy some prerequisites: four funeral cloths for each of the twenty mourners who would be chosen to accompany them, twenty sheep and twenty goats for the chief and some money for the musicians. Of course Dogo and Bonto saw no problem with those conditions. In fact the

items were doubled, because money was the least of the concerns of these two rich men. They were so relieved to be going to the funeral in style.

Dogo and Bonto left the palace happier than they had been in a long time. After their departure the council sat a little longer, selecting the 'mourners' and musicians. The party was made up of people who had their own axe to grind against the rich men. Some had lost their land to the men, while others' children had sustained dog bites when they had drifted too close to their mansions. A few others remembered the insults of these men just before they moved to their exclusive, newly-created neighbourhood. Furthermore, the party was schooled to abandon all conventions and dramatise the worst in them during the funeral rites.

When they arrived at the funeral grounds, the bereaved family was impressed by the expensive cloths which their in-laws wore, but that was all they could admire. They had immediate reason to change their moods. Instead of greeting anti clockwise, as was expected of them during such a formal occasion, the mourners greeted clockwise, all the while smiling broadly and looking very happy. In vain did others try to correct them. Soon after they sat down, they loudly complained of hunger, contrary to expected behaviour at a funeral. When they were provided with no food they brought out food which they had carried to the funeral grounds and started eating for all to see. They conversed and laughed noisily, cracking jokes about the poverty in the family of the deceased. An older man pointed out quite loudly that the family house of the rich man's wife leaked badly; once, he had had the misfortune of spending the night in that house and he could count all the stars in the sky just by looking through the gaping roof. An older woman, whose granddaughter had once been scared to death by Dogo's dogs, said for all to hear that one side of the roof of that house was supported by an old abandoned pestle.

Others proceeded to recount some of the weaknesses in the family of Dogo's wife, especially their inability to pay their debts, their farms which were competing with thorns for survival and the celebrated impotence of their men. You can imagine the embarrassment, anger and shock of the family and their guests.

The only person who was secretly happy about this sad turn of events was Dogo's wife's older sister. She rejoiced at the humiliation of her younger sister because ever since her marriage to a rich man she had shown no respect for her, and her arrogance had been encouraged by their mother who lost no opportunity to remind her of what a hopeless match she had made, married to that lazy palm wine tapper. Then she would praise the wealth and generosity of Dogo and end her harangue by thanking her soul for a daughter such as the one Dogo had married.

Dogo's wife, who wanted to die of shame, called Bonto to advise his friend to counsel his ill-mannered mourners, otherwise there would be trouble, more trouble than he would know what to do with. Dogo and Bonto for their part were so shocked that they did not even want people to know their true identities.

After the 'mourners' had finished eating and had attracted all the attention to themselves through their carefully orchestrated bulletins about the lives and times of the in-laws of a rich man, some brought out their musical instruments and played the happiest tunes ever heard at a funeral, while others danced and sang joyfully. In all, the solemn mood required while the body laid in state was abandoned, and the atmosphere was one of merrymaking. The more Dogo and Bonto tried to calm the 'mourners' the more excited they became and did the silliest of things, including singing 'dirges' with insulting lyrics and cracking more jokes about the clan of the bereaved. Dogo prayed hard that the earth would open and swallow him, and he wished with all his might that it was his own funeral he was witnessing, instead of such disgrace.

When the bereaved family could not take the insults any longer, they chased away the 'mourners', along with Dogo and Bonto.

The two headed straight for the palace of the chief and laid their complaint before him. The chief listened, with a smile on his face as the two rich men informed him of the behaviour of the mourners. After they had catalogued all their charges, the chief instructed his mediator to tell them that people can always acquire wealth if the times and the circumstances permit anyone to do so, and that anyone who became so rich as to think he or she could substitute human concern with wealth was just plain childish.

HOW KWEKU ANANSE WON THE HAND OF THE PRINCESS

A very long time ago, there lived in the animal kingdom a king who had a beautiful daughter called Okondor. She was beautiful and graceful, but she was causing her parents a lot of anxiety because she had turned down all offers of marriage. Okondor had dashed to the ground the hopes of numerous suitors, and one day her father the king decided that he was fed up by her indecision. The king told the inhabitants of the kingdom that whoever would be the first to bring a gourd of clean water from the spring and a gourd of fresh palm wine could have his daughter's hand in marriage.

Now the forest where the animals lived had the most refreshing spring water in the world, and it was also endowed with palm trees, but the forest was also

very dangerous. However, the animals received the challenge with enthusiasm and they entered the contest with a lot of zest because Okondor was worth any danger. They would all be so proud to be married to a woman that many men can only dream of.

The gourds were easy to come by, being the container in which water and wine were kept. However, the ease with which anyone could win the hand of the princess surprised the animals greatly. Hare wondered aloud:

"Why would anyone ask for a gourd of water and a gourd of wine in exchange for a young, beautiful woman like Princess Okondor?"

"I have often wondered how women must feel when they are reduced to such cheap commodities. Especially in the case of a princess. At least the king can do better than that?" Crab continued.

"Ah, Crab, you must swipe your mouth at the rubbish heap," admonished Cat.

"Why so? What abomination have I uttered?" enquired Crab.

"I agree with Cat," Duck cut in. "The way you expressed your views on marriage made it sound like females were of less value than males."

"Oh, I think you are all just overreacting. It does not take my views to make the female appear less important than the male. Just look around, and ask yourself which male wishes he were born female. But let me get to the point of this discussion. I have attended a number of marriages in this land, and I always wonder about the import of the bride price."

"I know that you are complaining because the male has to pay. How cheap you sound. You want everything for free! Why should a woman move into your house, cook and clean, work, give you children and daily pleasure all for free?" asked Cat.

"Yes, that is precisely the point. After the male has paid such a heavy bride price he feels entitled to something, doesn't he? If you ask me, I will tell you that the root of a lot of abuse of the female by the male stems from this practice," said Crab.

"I have deliberately kept quiet up until now," Tortoise contributed to the discussion. "But I hear that in other lands the female provides the bride price and still provides all the services our women provide, to the male."

"Really?" asked Turkey. "Then I should move into that land. Even the most inept males there must feel like lords indeed! Just imagine!"

"If what Tortoise says is true, then the bride price alone is not responsible for some of the unacceptable behaviour of some males in marriage. What I know is that some families see the marriage of their daughters as a chance to make money," said Squirrel.

"But then what does a king need? Only the poor and the greedy ask for heavy bride prices for their daughters. Some feel it will make the male treat the female better, but the evidence does not support the wish. Perhaps Okondor's constant refusal of suitors without giving any reasonable excuse is what is now annoying the king," mused Parrot. "Come to think of it, what else is there for her to do than to get married?"

"I know that everybody must get married someday," said Rat, "but we need to find out if our methods are really in the interest of all. The last time Mosquito's wife was obliged to go back to an abusive husband because her people could not return all the bride price. It was all the more difficult for her since Mosquito himself did not want a divorce."

"But the case of a princess like Okondor is different. Her people can refund the bride price any day. Who cannot return a gourd of water and a gourd of palm-wine?" asked Duiker.

"Perhaps that is the whole point. Maybe the king is using the marriage of his daughter to cause all of us to think over the matter of the procedure and details of marriage," concluded Tortoise who had decided not to waste his time in the contest because he moved so slowly.

While the discussion was going on Kweku Ananse just listened, keeping his thoughts to himself. He also felt that there was more to the contest than physical strength. He knew that no man in his right senses would ask men to compete over the hand of his daughter by asking them to race to the forest and bring water and palm wine. He felt it was a battle of the intellect. Certainly anyone could satisfy the king's requirements, but which of the animals had the intelligence to do it the fastest?

The debate continued among the animals until the appointed day, when the contestants headed for the forest to bring the water and the wine. Only the animals who could run the fastest entered the race, and these included Hare, Grass-cutter, Rat, Squirrel, Horse and Dog. Kweku Ananse the spider also entered as a contestant, and his presence just amused the others who knew that although he was wise, Ananse was physically weak, and that there was no way of him arriving first at the palace of the king with both gourds. Meanwhile, Ananse was also aware of his physical weakness and had devised a way of making the most of his mental capabilities, in order to outwit the stronger, faster contestants.

The animals dashed off into the forest to bring the requirements but even before Ananse could fill the first gourd with water, the others had completed both tasks and were already on their way to the palace. Ananse was not ruffled. He watched them run off as he took his time with the precious liquids.

He had come to the competition with a flute which he had carved out of a bamboo stem, and he started to play it. Ananse played so well that the other animals came back to find out where the music was coming from. Ananse told them that he got his singing bamboo flute from near the spring, and that there were a lot of singing flutes available for all of them too. Ananse told them that he planned to enter the palace of the king while playing the flute, in order to brighten his chances with Okondor who, they all knew, was very choosy. The animals, who had always believed in the reputed wisdom of Ananse, decided to do likewise.

Therefore, the animals went back to look for the singing bamboo flutes, leaving Ananse ahead of them in the race. It never occurred to any one of them that Ananse could get to the palace before them, and so they took their time. Meanwhile Ananse hurried towards the king's palace. After wasting quite a lot of time the other animals caught up with him and told him that there were no bamboo flutes at the spring. Ananse played another melodious tune for a while, before telling the other animals that he made a mistake the first time, and that the bamboo flutes could be found at the palm tree nearest to the spring.

Ananse took advantage of the gullibility of the animals and rested for a while before hurrying on his journey to win the hand of Okondor. When the animals caught up with him again, he was just a few hundred yards away from the palace, but the animals felt confident in their physical prowess and so when Ananse said that the flutes could be obtained at the palm tree farthest from the spring, they dashed away once again in search of a romantic touch to the contest.

Ananse thus strolled majestically to the palace of the king, where he was carried shoulder-high and was pronounced the husband of Okondor.

The other animals finally made it to the contest, too late. It was only then that they realised that Ananse had tricked them.

HOW THE CROW ACQUIRED HIS BLACK AND WHITE FEATHERS

A very long time ago there lived an old woman and her two grandchildren, Ampoma and Konadu. The old woman loved them very much. She cooked for them, played with them and in the evening, she told them interesting tales. She insisted, at all times, that the children must always tell the truth, no matter its consequences. Ampoma and Konadu also loved their grandmother, but what they did not like was that she was forever telling them things they should not do.

One day the old woman cooked their favourite dish, which was mashed yam mixed with palm oil and eaten with boiled eggs. After she had fed the children, she put her share in the bowl and left for the farm. Her grandchildren were too young to be of much help on the farm, so she usually left them at home, except during the time of harvesting. That day she had a lot of work to do and she knew they would only distract her with their endless questions. A little while after their grandmother left the house, Ampoma called Konadu:

"Konadu, I have an idea."

Konadu was curious. "Tell me about it."

"I think we should eat Nana's share of the food," Ampoma suggested.

"Why should we do that?"

"Why not? The food is really delicious and I want some more," explained Ampoma.

"I don't think that is a good idea. You know when Nana comes back she will be hungry. How are we going to explain what happened to her food?"

"I have thought of that. Remember the tale she told about Kweku Ananse and the water pot? We can also say that we cannot lift the pot and that we don't know who ate the food," suggested Ampoma.

"Well, I think we should eat only a little bit and leave some for Nana," Konadu compromised her honesty.

The children went and brought the bowl and ate a small portion of the mashed yam and one egg. Then they rearranged the food in the bowl, covered it and placed it where it belonged. After a while they went back to the bowl and ate some more, rearranged the rest of the food and covered the bowl like they had done before.

This continued until there was no more food to be rearranged. The bowl was empty, but they covered it anyway and went about their chore of picking the stones from the dried beans. They agreed to deny any knowledge of what had happened to the food.

When Nana came from the farm she was tired and famished. She placed a bunch of firewood she had brought with her on the floor, and gave Konadu and Ampoma some guavas and tangerines. Seeing how generous she was despite her obvious fatigue, Ampoma and Konadu immediately regretted eating their grandmother's food. She went to have a cool bath and, sitting on her stool just outside of her door, she called Ampoma to bring her bowl of food.

"Nana," Ampoma called from the kitchen, "the bowl is so heavy that I cannot pick it up."

"Which bowl? I just want the bowl of mashed yam and boiled eggs. How can that be too heavy? Konadu, please go and bring me my food," Nana instructed Konadu.

"Nana," Konadu also called her grandmother," Ampoma is right. The bowl is too heavy. I cannot pick it up either."

Nana got up with a lot of difficulty, went into the room and brought the bowl which felt even lighter that she remembered. Then she asked for water and washed her hands, while Ampoma and Konadu watched her from the window, their hearts pounding. They hid their faces as Nana opened the bowl and found it empty.

"Ampoma! Konadu Come here at once!!" she ordered the two children. "Now I know why the pot was too heavy. Which of you ate the food? Or did both of you eat it? And why did you not simply say so? I could have cooked something else for myself."

Nana was very angry, not so much because the children had eaten the food, but because they had planned to lie about it. What made matters worse was that both Ampoma and Konadu adamantly denied any knowledge of the food's disappearance. They even agreed to go with Nana to the Goddess of the river to find out who the real culprit was.

When the three of them got to the river, it was very shallow. Nana took out a raw egg and invoked the river Goddess to help her solve a big mystery and instil honesty in her grandchildren. After the prayer she threw the egg into the river and called Ampoma to step inside. Then she taught her a song and instructed her to sing it three times:

If I am the one who ate Nana's yam,
If I am the one who ate Nana's eggs,
If I have planned with my sister

To lie about the yam and the eggs,

If I have planned with my sister

To lie about the yam and the eggs,

Then River Goddess, carry me away,

Oh, river, carry me far away.

After singing the song for the first time, the river rose to Ampoma's knees. The end of the second time saw the river at her waist line, and after the third song, the river rose just below her nose. Nana was satisfied that Ampoma was guilty. Do you think Konadu had the sense to own up even at this time? No! She insisted that she never ate the food, so Nana offered the same prayer and Konadu stepped into another part of the river which was shallow, and she started singing:

If I am the one who ate Nana's yam,

If I am the one who ate Nana's eggs,

If I have planned with my sister

To lie about the yam and the eggs,

If I have planned with my sister

To lie about the yam and the eggs,

Then River Goddess, carry me away,

Oh, river, carry me far away.

By the time she sang the song three times the river had covered all but Konadu's eyes. Then Nana started to panic because she did not want to lose her grandchildren who were about to be drowned. She tried to enter the river but it was already overflowing its banks. She frantically called out to Ampoma and Konadu but they were moving farther and farther away from her. The river was really carrying them away! She turned round frantically and saw the crow perched on the tree just behind her, watching the whole episode.

"Crow, you must really help me. All I wanted was to teach my grandchildren a lesson. I did not mean to lose them. They are all I have for relatives. They are the children of my only daughter who died while having her third child. Crow, please help me before the river carries them away. How can I tell their mother when I meet her in the spirit world that her children did not live long because of boiled yam and eggs?"

Nana started to cry, and Crow had pity on her.

"Nana, I will save your grandchildren" Crow assured the old woman. "But how are you going to repay me?"

"If you are able to save my grandchildren, I will give you my most prized possession. I own a small piece of white fabric and a bigger piece of black broadcloth which are part of my family's heirloom. You can have both of them. But please hurry up or the river will take them away," Nana pleaded.

Crow flew to the river and picked up the children, one at a time, with his beak and brought them to the bank. Nana wept with joy and the children finally understood that it is not worth telling lies, especially to people who love you. On the way to the house Crow advised Nana never to resort to such harsh measures when dealing with children, because that can harden them and worse, can be fatal.

Crow greatly admired the two pieces of cloth. He wore the black one from his shoulders down to his feet while reserving a small piece for a head kerchief. He used the white piece as a scarf around his neck. He never took them off.

HOW SOME ANIMALS CAME TO BE DOMESTICATED

Today we can see that some animals live at home while others live only in the forest, but this has not always been so. A long time ago, all the animals lived in the forest, and only the hunter could kill any and bring it home for food. During this time, Dog, Lion, Goat, Leopard and Cat lived in the same house and they did everything together, including hunting, cooking and taking care of each other.

Leopard and Lion were great hunters, Dog and Cat not as good. So whenever Leopard and Lion brought the day's catch, Dog and Cat would skin the animal and smoke it. Goat had no skill with hunting and so his job was to gather mushrooms and vegetables, and to uproot some yams and cassava. As well, Goat was in charge of the cooking. This arrangement worked quite well until Leopard started to feel cheated. He saw that Goat was growing very well with good, strong muscles and a shiny coat. Leopard felt that Goat owed his handsomeness to the efforts of others who brought home such tasty meat every day.

"Surely, Goat would not have grown so well if he only survived on the mushrooms and cassava. He owes his weight and good looks to the risk that some of us take trying to catch game for his meals. I think Goat will taste really delicious, given all that he eats," Leopard told himself and began trying to find a way of getting rid of Goat.

Leopard finally discussed the matter secretly with Lion and they called a meeting of all the inhabitants of the house, being Dog, Cat, Goat and the two of them. Leopard spoke first:

"Friends, I think that Goat takes us all for fools. Not even small fools but big fools."

Dog and Cat were surprised at the utterance of Leopard, while Goat went into a state of shock.

"Let me explain what I mean: I know that Dog and Cat do not have much strength but they are seen trying to hunt once in a while. I remember the mice and lizards which Cat brings and the weasel which Dog brought only last week. Goat makes no effort at all. He just goes nearby and uproots mushrooms and cassava and he believes that will continue to satisfy us. This will simply not do!"

Dog and Cat tried to intervene by saying meekly that they would double their efforts in order to help Goat out, but neither Lion nor Leopard would hear of the suggestion. At the end of the meeting the order was given that Goat produce, within five days, some game if he did not want to end up as game. Confused and terrified, Goat started wailing:

"O mother, my mother,
You know my plight!
The path confronting me
Is thorny indeed
Mother, mother you have
Been away too long
Alas! Alas!
Mother, I hope you are not sleeping,
That you can see me now.
Life is such a struggle
There is no refuge anywhere..."

Although Dog and Cat felt sorry for Goat, they were afraid of expressing their solidarity with him, and so they watched and silently grieved for the plight of their friend. In the end, Goat had no choice but to comply with the order.

The following day Goat set off to find game in the forest. He was not used to the deep forest and he had no idea where to start. The trees stood tall and imposing, their branches forming a canopy which blocked the sun and the sky. It looked like the forest never experienced sunlight and Goat found the atmosphere strange indeed. The only noises he could hear were the chirping of the birds, the screeching of the crickets and the near-silent trickle of a stream. He wondered if there were any other animals this deep in the forest. He had thought it was a matter simply of walking to find game waiting to be picked.

Knowing that his life was at stake, Goat kept walking through the forest until he met Donkey to whom he narrated his plight. And come to think of it, Donkey is the cousin of Goat. Goat being not so smart informed Donkey that he would take him home as game, whereupon Donkey began to run away, with Goat in pursuit.

Both started the run in the morning, and even when the sun got ready to retire for the day they were still running. After a while both of them were exhausted.

Tortoise had been watching the two of them all day, trying to figure out what kind of game they were engaged in. He moved away from his hiding spot and called Goat:

"Hey! Goat! Why have you been running all day after your cousin the donkey?"

Goat stopped, took a deep breath and said:

"My lord, Tortoise, I am in such deep trouble at home."

"Why, what is the problem?"

"Hmm. I live with Lion, Leopard, Dog and Cat. They know very well that I do not have strong paws for hunting, and that my horns are not very effective for the job either. Yet they insist that if I fail to produce game within five days I will end up as the meat for the day's soup."

"Why did they come to such a decision? What is your role in the house? Do you just eat and sleep?" Tortoise tried to understand how Goat's own cotenants could have arrived at such a remarkable decision.

"Since I cannot hunt, I gather the vegetable and snails; I uproot cassava and yams and I also do the cooking and clean the house. Yet they feel I do not do enough to measure up to their hunting abilities. So, Tortoise, I am so desperate that I'd chase even my own cousin for meat in order to save my life," Goat explained.

"Oh I see, so chasing him all day is your idea of hunting! I thought you were involved in some kind of competition or that you had bet on something."

"How can I catch an animal for meat if I don't chase it?" asked Goat, genuinely confused.

"Well in the first place, no matter how desperate you get, the first rule is that you do not kill your own. What you need is a gun or a weapon like a sharpened, strong stick. But don't you worry about that. I have a magic stone, and you can use it for a while."

"Oh, Tortoise, how can I thank you?" asked Goat.

"You don't need to worry about that either. I heard you wail for your dead mother sometime ago and her ghost instructed me to help you, so listen carefully," continued Tortoise. "You only need to throw this stone at any animal you see and it will die instantly. Just remember not to kill another goat or any of your relatives. The animals are not used to seeing you hunt and so they will make little effort to avoid you. Don't start chasing them like you chased the donkey, or else they'll be suspicious. Act normally, and call them in your usual voice. They'll think you just want to chat with them, and when they are close enough, throw the stone at them and you see what will happen. You will carry so much meat home that the people you live with will even feel ashamed for harassing you so."

At first Goat was not sure of the efficacy of the stone but he decided to try it, because time was running out. Also, he had always known that his mother would never cease to look out for him, even beyond the grave. Shortly after leaving Tortoise, Goat saw a turkey pecking away at some dried bean pods. Goat walked at his habitual manner towards the bird and called him:

"Turkey, my friend, how is the day going?"

Turkey turned round and started to hop towards Goat who immediately threw the magic stone at the bird. Turkey stopped in his tracks, turned to the left and to the right, and fell on his back, dead.

Goat picked up the animal and placed it in a basket which he had woven out of palm branches. In a similar manner Goat found a rabbit, a duiker, a pig, a grass-cutter and even a monkey. He was so excited that he looked up to the sky and the earth and offered a prayer of gratitude to the Sky God and Mother Earth. Notwithstanding his excitement, he had a hard time carrying the basket home, and so he dragged it until he came to the crossroads. Here he picked the rabbit and the grass-cutter and went home to ask for help.

When he got home the others still voiced doubt about Goat's ability to bring home any game, but they decided to find out for themselves. They accompanied Goat to the crossroads, and they could not help but express their amazement at the variety and quantity of meat that they saw. They feasted for several days and Goat did not feel threatened any more, until Lion had another thought.

Lion told Leopard that if they did not find out how Goat killed his animals, very soon Goat would seize power from the two of them. "I have observed how he has been prancing about these days and feeling so confident," Leopard cautioned Lion.

"I am not surprised. His eyeballs are clearly moving beyond his eyebrows, as the elders express it. Just imagine – the last time I asked him for a calabash of water he asked me to fetch it for myself. A month ago he would have brought the water even before the words were out of my mouth," said Lion.

"Since his discovered ability to trap meat he has become impossible to live with. I also asked him two days ago what we were going to have for lunch and do you know what Goat asked me? I will tell you. He wanted to know if I were made of wax and why I don't go near the fire and start the cooking!! It was not so much what he said as how he said it. Talk of impertinence! I wonder if we did the right thing by asking him to hunt for meat instead of gathering the vegetables and doing the cooking." Leopard was getting upset. He agreed that they should discover the tricks of Goat, and that Cat be used as the informant. The two of them called Cat when Goat and Dog had gone for a walk. Lion spoke:

"Cat, we have something important to tell you. We have observed that among all of us you are the one who can keep secrets best. Dog is a plain fool, or he would not make babies in broad daylight for the whole world to referee his performance. We cannot trust Dog, but we trust you. Tomorrow it will be the turn of Goat to hunt for meat. We want you to follow him to the forest and find out how he does it."

Cat expressed his misgivings about the assignment. "Why is that important? After all, through his efforts we all have more than enough meat at any given time."

"Cat, have you not seen how Goat has been carrying himself lately? If we are not careful, one of these fine days he will place himself in a position of authority above us all; then what will happen to us?" Leopard asked Cat.

Cat understood that it was futile to argue with the two beasts. More than this, he also knew how ruthless they could be. The dirge Goat had sung when given the order to produce game or lose his life had never left Cat's mind, and he had since

123

then been feeling uncomfortable in the house, knowing that he could be singled out for a similar ordeal. He told Lion and Leopard that he would spy on Goat and let them know the outcome.

At dawn, soon after Goat had left for the forest, Cat woke Dog.

"Dog, wake up!"

"Why? It is not even daybreak."

"I know. But you must get up immediately."

"What is wrong?"

"It is important that we go hunting with Goat."

"Is that the new rule? No one goes hunting with me, so why should I go hunting with Goat?"

"By the time you finish asking all those questions Lion and Leopard would have come for you," Dog told Cat.

When Dog had rubbed the sleep away from his eyes, Cat told him that he had overheard Lion and Leopard planning to kill the three of them. Upon hearing this information Dog quickly roused himself from his sleeping mat and they followed Goat's tracks till they saw him at a distance.

Goat was indeed surprised to find the two of them. Cat explained what the trouble was all about. The three of them thought and debated for a long time until they concluded if they did not kill Lion and Leopard they would know no peace; worst, the two huge beasts would reduce them to slavery, which is a slow kind of death. In their wanderings they met a hunter to whom they narrated their story. The hunter said:

"I fail to see why you are so afraid. Goat, you already have the solution. Take the magic stone which Tortoise gave you and get rid of these pests in the same way as you have been killing your game. I will go with you." Hunter, Cat and Dog watched from a distance while Goat walked into the house. Lion was the first he found. He wanted to know if he brought home any meat. Goat told him that he was tired of hunting meat and that he had decided to eat vegetables from then on. Lion got so angry at this reply that he called Leopard to witness the insolence of Goat.

"Goat, what catch did you bring today?" asked Leopard who soon joined them.

"What catch? Do I look like your servant? I was doing well with vegetables until you forced me to become a hunter. I am tired of hunting and I am not taking your stupid orders anymore."

No sooner were these words out of Goat's mouth than the two huge beasts moved to pounce on Goat. But, instead of grabbing him, they both fell back, too weak to move. Then Hunter, Dog and Cat emerged from behind the mango tree from where they were watching the drama. Hunter took his gun and finished them off.

They all removed the skins off the animals and dried their meat over fire. They carried the meat and moved away from the forest in order to live with hunter who had become their friend.

From that day onwards animals like Goat, Dog and Cat have always lived near man, for fear of vengeance from the relatives of the lion and the leopard.